All rights reserved. Published by Scholastic Inc., *Publishers since 1920.*
SCHOLASTIC and associated logos are trademarks and/or registered trademarks of Scholastic Inc.

The publisher does not have any control over and does not assume any responsibility for author or third-party websites or their content.

This book is a work of fiction. Names, characters, places, and incidents are either the product of the author's imagination or are used fictitiously, and any resemblance to actual persons, living or dead, business establishments, events, or locales is entirely coincidental.

ISBN 978-1-338-78730-6

10 9 8 7 6 5 4 3 2 1   21 22 23 24 25
Printed in Mexico
First printing 2021

Art by Keiron Ward for Artful Doodlers Ltd.
Book Design by Heather Daugherty

LIFE IS BETTER WITH
F·R·I·E·N·D·S
THE TELEVISION SERIES

By Micol Ostow

Scholastic Inc.

Life is better with friends.

There are many kinds of friends.

Monica is the foodie friend!
She's loyal, caring, and **very** organized. (Most of the time.)

Chandler is the funny friend!
He's the best buddy to have. He's reliable and loves to hang out. Even if he's in the bath.

Ross is a **dyno-mite** friend!
He's smart, dependable, and a loving big brother to Monica.

Rachel is the fashionable friend!
She's spunky, stylish, and marches to the beat of her own drum.

Phoebe is the free-spirited friend!
She's quirky and loves to sing. (She's also always got your back.)

Joey is the famous friend!
He plays Dr. Drake Ramoray on a TV show. Joey is goofy and
enjoys the spotlight, but his friends always come first.

These six pals all know:
Life is so much better with friends!

Friends can be fancy.

Friends can be silly.

Friends can be furry . . .

fluffy . . .

or . . . not.

Sometimes they can even be . . . smelly!

Parties are **always** better with friends.

Especially when they're pizza parties!

Vacations are better with friends.

And vacation **problems** are better with friends, too.

OUCH!

Even if it's a rainy day.

Friends make treats.

Friends eat treats.

(Even when you'd rather they didn't.)

Holidays are better with friends.

But maybe not holiday food!
(Always read the recipe!)

Even doing the laundry is better with friends!

Moving furniture?
Definitely better with friends.

Friends might not always agree . . .

. . . and things can get a little complicated.

But true friends know how
to make things right.

Just ask Chandler about the time he spent
six hours in a box as an apology to Joey.
(Saying "I'm sorry" often works, too!)

Snacks are better with friends.

But always remember!
Some friends don't share food.

"JOEY DOESN'T SHARE FOOD!"

Naps are better with friends.

Friends know you better than anyone else . . . most of the time!

Even if you're just hanging out . . .

. . . everything is better when you're with friends.

Friends are the family
we choose for ourselves.

Do you have a friend who's special to you?
Tell them:

"YOU'RE MY LOBSTER!"

"TOGETHER IS BETTER!"

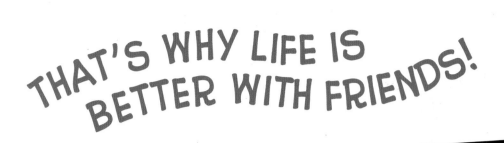